# GARAGE SONG

WRITTEN BY
## SARAH WILSON

ILLUSTRATED BY
## BERNIE KARLIN

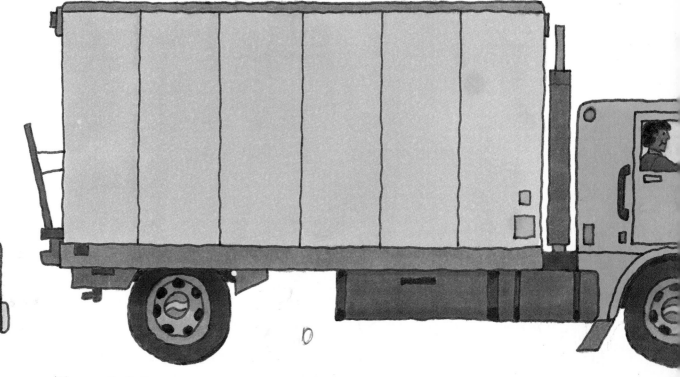

**Simon & Schuster Books for Young Readers**
Published by Simon & Schuster, New York • London • Toronto • Sydney • Tokyo • Singapore

SIMON & SCHUSTER BOOKS FOR YOUNG READERS
Simon & Schuster Building, Rockefeller Center
1230 Avenue of the Americas, New York, New York 10020

Designed by Bernie Karlin.
The text of this book is set in Bookman.
Manufactured in the United States of America.

10 9 8 7 6 5 4 3 2 1

Library of Congress Cataloging-in-Publication Data
Wilson, Sarah. Garage song/by Sarah Wilson:
illustrated by Bernie Karlin.
Summary: A boy spends a day watching the men at work
at a busy service station.
[1. Automobiles—service stations—Fiction. 2. Stories in rhyme.]
I. Karlin, Bernie, ill. II. Title. 91-393 AC  PZ8.3.W698Gar  1991 [E]—dc20
ISBN: 0-671-73565-9

For Kay and John Remington
and their home garage of wonders;
also for mechanics
Herb, Elizabeth, and Homer.

**SW**

For Morris and Harry.
Thanks to
Carl, Ted, Frank, Barbara, Shirley,
Howie's station,
and my wife Mati.

**BK**

Early in the morning sun,
doors roll up and hoses run —
*splish* and *splash*
and *gush* and *sputter* —
through the garage and pavement gutter.

Pumps are open once again.
"Hi ya!" say the station men,
Fred and Jim and, later, Mike.
"Need some help, son, with your bike?
Tires look low. Let's give them air.
Wheel it over. Park it there."

*Pssssssst, pssssssst, pssssssst!*
The air hose hisses.
Fills my bike tires,
never misses!

Then — *brrrrrum, brrrrrum* —
the first car comes
with engine squeaks
and creaks and hums.

Behind it follow seven more!
Tools clink-clank upon the floor.

"Get this trunk, Jim, I'll unlatch it!"
"Here's a hose, Mike. Let's attach it!"
*Click, click, click* and wiggle-a-stick.
"Rewiring there will do the trick!"

Zapa-zapa-zapa SHOOSH!
Someone's wiper blade is loose.
Rucket-a, rucket-a — hubcap's gone.
Old tire's off and new tire's on!

"Oil for the gears, son?
  Pedals too?"
A wash and a wipe
and my bike looks new!

At noon as cars zoom zoom around,
the garage fills up with sun and sound:

shake, shake, shake
and *bang, bang, bang.*
*Rattle, rattle, rumble*
and *clang, clang, CLANG!*
*Bing, bing, bang*
and *beep, beep, honk!*

*Screech, screech, screech* and
*thrummmmm, thrummmmm, BONK!*
*Swoosh-a-little, whoosh-a-little,*
*snort, snort, grrrrrrrrr!*
Then around the corner comes
*purrrrrr, purrrrrr, purrrrrr!*

Cars zoom in and out and in
to fill with gas and leave again —
chug-chug chargers, big rear-enders,
old put-putters, dent-in-fenders;
slickered cars all shined and waxy;
wagons, vans, and there's a taxi!

Time to take a break at three
for Fred and Jim and Mike and me.
Cans shoot out in red and green —
*clunkety THUNK* — from the soda machine.

Fred takes two
and I take one.
We sit and drink them
in the sun,

as trucks roll by and shake the ground,
go up the street to turn around,
and roar back in with braking *squeals*,
like giant houses
propped on wheels!

Work goes on from early dawn
and then toward dusk the lights switch on.
Tools are stowed away from sight.
Brooms go sweeping left to right,

while sunset clouds drift through the sky,
and Fred and Jim both wave goodbye.
Mike stays on, but sharp at ten,
he'll roll the garage doors shut again.

I'm off, too. It's early June
and time for supper. "See you soon!"

Shadows lengthen.
Dark is falling.
From the fields,
small owls are calling.
Crickets join them
in a song.

Far-off engines hum along.

There I leave you on my bike,
Painted in your pool of light,
small oasis, neon-bright.

Little garage, good night.
Good night.